GOOD MORNING
DANNY

Dale and Al Carlson   Atheneum   New York

This is a boy.
His name is Danny.
He is nearly three years old.
He is strong, like you are,
and getting bigger every day.
Say, "Good morning, Danny."

This is Danny's city.
He lives in an apartment.

When he looks out of his window
what does he see?

But Danny is still asleep.
Tell him to wake up.

Danny's bear is very lazy.
Tell him to wake up, too.

This is Danny's breakfast.
What do you eat for breakfast?

Hurry up and drink
your milk, Danny.

It's time to go to the playground.
Danny rides his bicycle next to his mother.
The cars and buses are noisy.

The policeman, the fireman,
and the butcher wave to Danny.
People are hurrying everywhere.

In the playground, Danny pedals his bicycle very fast.
The wheels go around and around.

The sandbox has railings
and steps that go down.

Danny goes down and what does he do?
He fills his pail like you.

There is a big slide and a small slide.
Which is the right size for Danny?

Danny likes the small swing best.
It just fits him and there is a bar
across the front so he won't fall out.

When the snow falls, it makes
the whole city white.
The houses are white, the cars are white,
the park is white. Danny makes a snowman.

This is Danny's sled.
Sometimes he stays on the sled, sometimes not.

Whose bathrobe and slippers
are these? Are they Danny's?
They belong to Danny's father.
But Danny likes to try them on.
They don't fit yet, but they will someday.

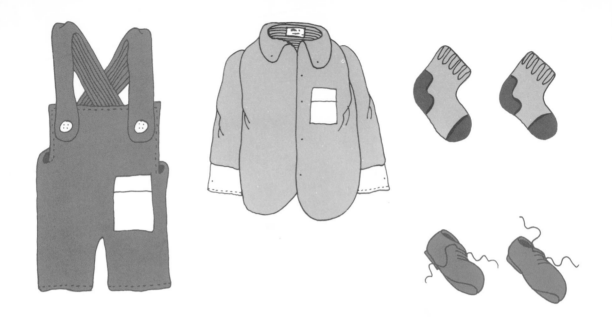

These are Danny's clothes.
One shirt, one pair of pants,
two socks, and two shoes.

Mommy puts them on Danny in the morning.
But Danny can take them off at night by himself.

Danny brushes his teeth.
So does bear.

Danny takes bear to bed
because he is soft and friendly.
Who do you take to bed?

Night has come to Danny's city.
The sky is dark. The houses are dark.

But the moon is bright
and so is the light,
the small night light in Danny's room.

Look in Danny's window.
Say good night to Danny.
But not too loudly,
because Danny is asleep.

"Good night, Danny."